A day with the
Animal Doctors

Sharon Rentta

Today Terence is feeling
Especially Important.
He is going to be a doctor.

His mommy's going to be a doctor, too, like she always is.

Dr. Terence packs his
First Aid Kit.

HOSPITAL

PHYSICAL THERAPY

WARD

OPERATING ROOM

X-RAY

BANDAGE ROOM

ENTRANCE

Then he shows Mommy
the way to the hospital.
Hospitals are Very Busy.

There are lots of patients in the waiting room.
Waiting can be quite Boring . . .

. . . so Dr. Terence shows them
his best dance moves.

Everyone feels much better after that,

except for the cleaning mice.

Some patients
need to see a doctor.

There's Dr. Yak,

Dr. Zebra,

Dr. Chimp,

Dr. Mommy

and

Dr. Terence.

All the doctors have tails except Dr. Chimp.

These are some of the things that doctors use to make people better:

a stethoscope,

a bandage,

a watch,

a syringe,

a thermometer

and a nice cup of tea.

They also use Bedside Manner, which means being nice to people. Dr. Terence has an Especially Good Bedside Manner.

Some patients need to see a nurse.

This is Nurse Glenda.

When patients have gotten stuck in things,

Nurse Glenda is very good
at getting them unstuck.

This is Nurse Steve.

Sometimes Nurse Steve
needs help with
the bandages.

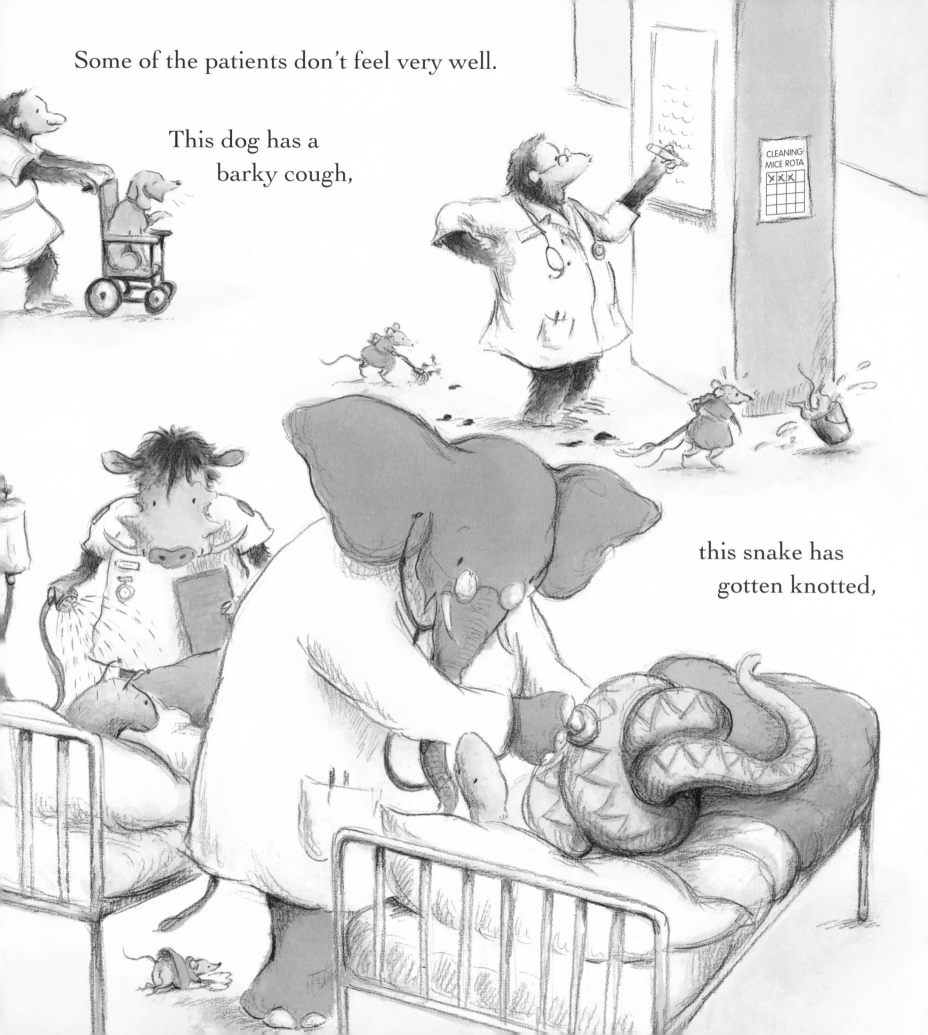

Some of the patients don't feel very well.

This dog has a
barky cough,

this snake has
gotten knotted,

and this leopard has
lost his spots.

It takes ages to sweep them all up.

Some of the patients have had accidents.

This giraffe cricked his neck
looking around a sharp corner.

This koala fell out of a tree
when he was asleep.

And this dog swallowed
an alarm clock.

Tick!
Tock!

He's going to have an x-ray.

An x-ray is a special photograph that shows what's going on inside you.

What's going on inside
this dog is a lot of ticking.

Tick!
Tock!

When the patients get hungry, Dr. Terence helps out with the food.

These are some of the things the patients eat:

bananas

slugs
(for the frogs)

sausages

carrots

dog food

dessert

Doctors like a snack, too.

Dr. Yak says he's exhausted, and the day's only halfway through.

Some of the patients are really old. They sleep a lot, watch television, and knit. Then they tell Dr. Terence about what it was like when they were little.

Then they fall asleep again.

This crocodile has
lost his false teeth.

Some patients are waiting to be born:

tadpoles
2 weeks

ant
2 weeks

crocodile
12 weeks

snake
12 weeks

chicken
3 weeks

goose
4 weeks

seagull
4 weeks

duck
4 weeks

ostrich
6 weeks

Some patients have only just been born.

Dr. Terence sings the babies a lullaby.

Some of the patients are very big.

They can make the Biggest Fuss.

Some patients are only little.
They often need to do a lot of Bouncing.

It's important for doctors to do Bouncing, too.

But sometimes
even doctors can
have accidents.

Then they need three things:

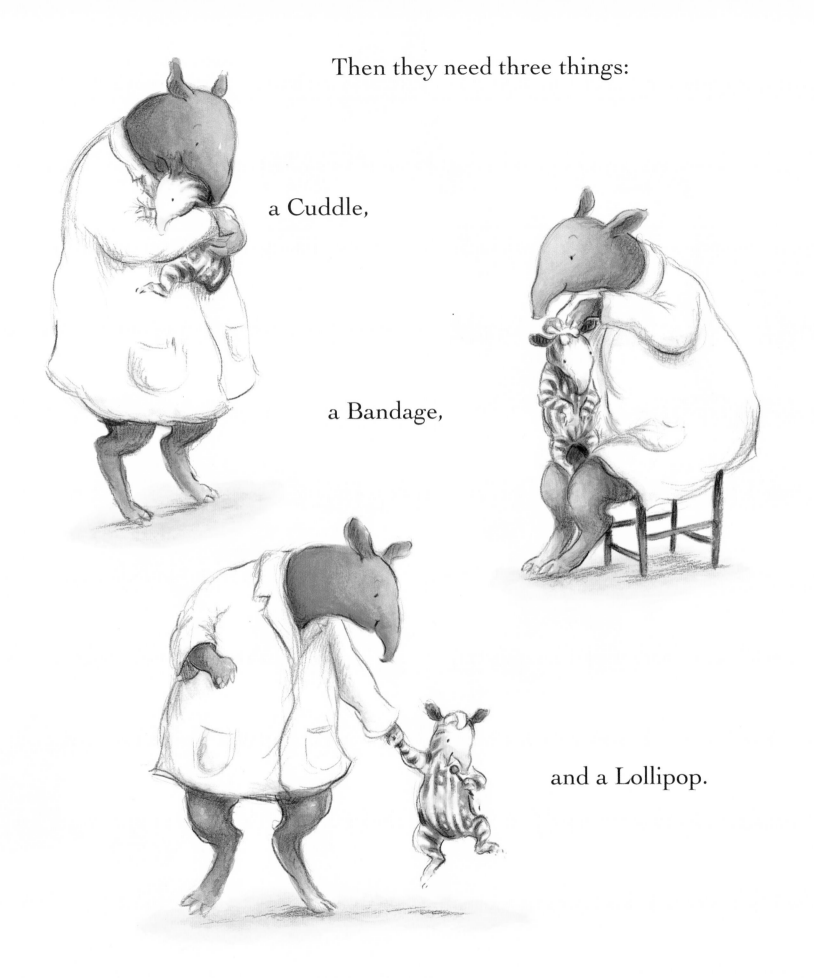

a Cuddle,

a Bandage,

and a Lollipop.

At the end of a long day,
doctors get tired. Then
they have to go home . . .

EXIT

for a bath,

and a bedtime story.

But a good doctor is
never really off duty.

It's hard work being a doctor.

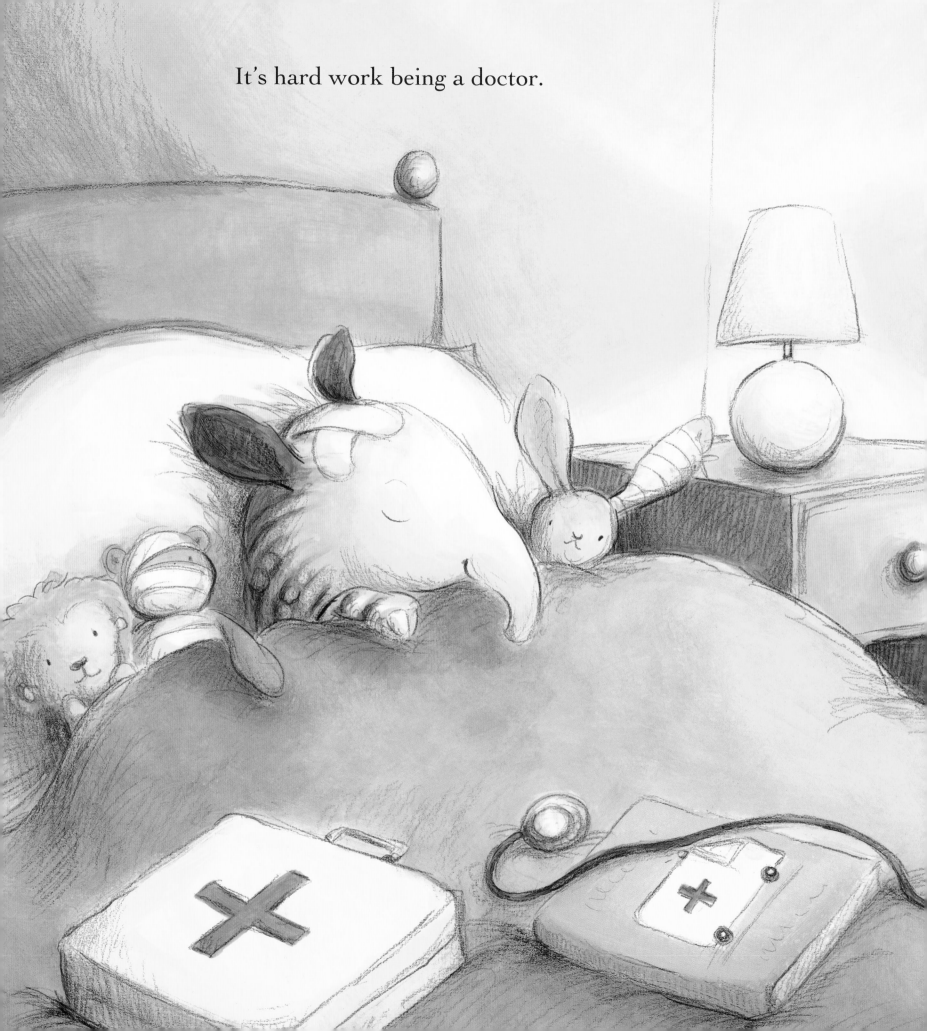

Night-night, Dr. Terence.

For the Hori family,
and for Dr. Li Tee,
and Nurse Ginny

First published in 2011 by Alison Green Books
An imprint of Scholastic Children's Books
Euston House, 24 Eversholt Street
London NW1 1DB
A division of Scholastic Ltd
London ~ New York ~ Toronto ~ Sydney
Auckland ~ Mexico City ~ New Delhi ~ Hong Kong

ISBN 978-1-4351-4867-3

Manufactured in Malaysia
 Lot #:
 9 8 7 6 5 4 3 2
 April 2014